BYE, PENGUIN!

Seou Lee

LQ

LEVINE QUERIDO

MONTCLAIR · AMSTERDAM · NEW YORK

This is an Em Querido book
Published by Levine Querido

LQ
LEVINE QUERIDO

www.levinequerido.com • info@levinequerido.com

Levine Querido is distributed by Chronicle Books LLC

Text and illustrations copyright © 2020 by Seou Lee
Originally published in Korea by BookGoodCome

Library of Congress Control Number: 2019955258
ISBN 978-1-64614-021-3

Printed and bound in China

Published in October 2020
First Printing

Book design by Christine Kettner
The text type was set in Just Tell Me What.

Seou Lee created the illustrations digitally using Photoshop and a Wacom tablet.

Craaaack

Snick!

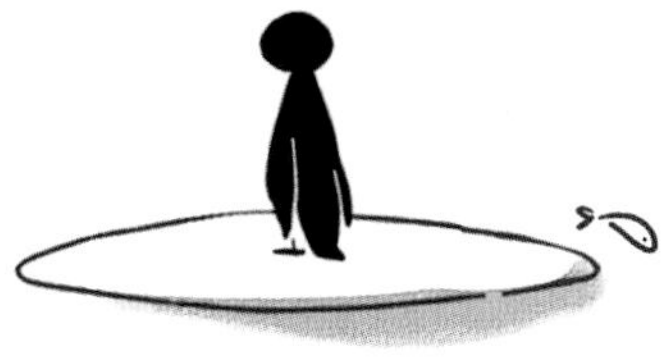